D1475092

"I'm Afraid of the Vampire State Building"

Also by Patti Greenberg Wollman

Behind the Playdough Curtain:
A Year in My Life as a Preschool Teacher

Brandi, age 6

"I'm Afraid of the
Vampire
State
Building"
Wit and Wisdom from
the Two-to-Seven Set

Patti Greenberg Wollman
and Merril Feinstein-Feit

Golden Books · New York

Ashley, age 6

Golden Books®

888 Seventh Avenue
New York, NY 10106

Thank you to the kids at P.S. 63 in Manhattan and
the other kids who drew art for this book.

Copyright © 1997 by Patti Greenberg Wollman and Merril Feinstein-Feit
All rights reserved, including the right of reproduction in whole or in part in any form.
Golden Books® and colophon are trademarks
of Golden Books Publishing Co., Inc.
Designed by Anna Raff
Manufactured in the United States of America

10 9 8 7 6 5 4 3 2 1

Library of Congress Cataloging-in-Publication Data   .

Wollman, Patti Greenberg.
        I'm afraid of the Vampire State Building / Patti Greenberg Wollman
and Merril Feinstein-Feit.
            p.   cm.
        ISBN 0-307-44018-4 (alk. paper)
        1. Children — Quotations.   I. Feinstein-Feit, Merril.   II. Title.
PN6328.C5W65   1997
081' .083—dc21
97-6867

To my family—Warren, Laura, and Benjy—
the source of my joy and strength

P. G. W.

To Stu, Sam, and my pew-mates,
with love and respect

M. F. F.

Introduction

What do children do all day? Their main job is to make sense of the world. This is not an easy task. Children share the same feelings as the adults who care for them, but they're not old enough to think the same thoughts. The only way they can ask questions or explain themselves is by using our common tool: language.

Like umpires, children call it as they see it—they interpret their knowledge in a very literal sense. Their comments can be charming, poignant, or hilarious. More important, a child's words can open a window of understanding for his grown-up listener.

As preschool teachers, we spent a year collecting these small jewels. As mothers, we supplied some of these anecdotes ourselves. We offer them to you. Prepare to enjoy yourself as you come with us into the enchanting world of early childhood!

Four-year-old Isaac didn't want to go on a field trip to midtown Manhattan. When his mother asked him the reason, Isaac said, "I'm afraid of the Vampire State Building."

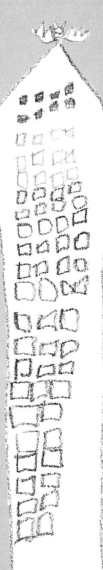

Brandi, age 6

Simón, age 6

Three-year-old Bridget asked her mother,
"If a clock has $\mathtt{hands}$, why can't it clap?"

Rebecca, age 8

Three-year-old Martin asked his mother, "Why are you my 𝔪𝔬𝔪𝔪𝔶?"

"Because you grew in my tummy," she told him.

"How did I eat?" he asked.

She patiently explained that he was fed through an umbilical cord. Martin thought for a minute. Then he smiled brightly. "I know! On the end of the umbilical cord there must have been a 𝔣𝔬𝔯𝔨!"

It was the beginning of nursery school, during the adjustment period. Three-year-old Lillie was ready to play in her classroom, but her father was having difficulty saying good-bye. Finally, the little girl put her hands on her hips, rolled her eyes, and told him, "I'm all adjusted now, Daddy. Even if you go down the hall to the coffee room and wait for me to visit you, I won't come. So you should just go home now."

Anthony, age 7

Six-year-old Aaron asked his mother what was for dinner. "Chicken soup," answered his mother.

"My favorite food—

thank God!" said Aaron excitedly.

"Why are you thanking God?" his mother wanted to know. "*I* made the chicken soup."

"Yeah," said Aaron, "but God made the chicken."

A three-year-old woke his mother early one **morning**.
"Mommy, are you a little bit up?"

She opened one eye. "Jared, what have you been eating?"

"Nothing!" he protested. "Does it look
like chocolate?"

Liviya, age 8

Three-year-old Jordan told his mother, "You know what people are made of? Bones and muscles and kisses and hugs."

Richie, age 6

Two three-year-olds were deciding whether they wanted to go to the playground with their mothers. Melissa said she was afraid of bees. "That's all right," said Jason reassuringly. "They only care about flowers."

Laura was a two-and-a-half-year-old city kid who loved to go to the park. One day her mother told her that they were going to Florida to visit her grandparents.

Laura had only one question: "Do they have grass?"

Micaela, age 9

A mother went into her five-year-old's room to awaken him for school. Still in bed, he began to talk to her about buying a puppet and putting on a show. "Alex, what are you talking about?" his mother inquired.

Alex opened his eyes. "Oh, Mommy," he exclaimed, "you got out of my dream before I did!"

A kindergarten teacher was walking on the beach one morning, collecting shells for her class. A worried young boy approached her. "Lady," he said, pointing to the shells still on the beach, "are you gonna take them all?"

Alex, age 6

Four-year-old Sophie was watching the wind blow through the leaves on a tree. "Look, Mommy," she exclaimed. "The leaves are waving to Heaven!"

Five-year-old Rachel went to court with her lawyer father. The judge asked her if she knew what a burglar was. "Yes," she declared. "That's a robber who steals burgers."

Hilla, age 9

14

Four-year-old Danny was looking at black-and-white pictures of his mother's childhood in Brooklyn. He wanted to know only one thing: "Do they have colors in Brooklyn?"

A teacher came into a classroom, spoke to the teacher there, and left the room. Five-year-old Allison remarked,

"I love the smell of the perfume that lady was wearing."

Her friend Dennis replied, "Oh, I didn't smell anything. I guess I'm deaf in my nose."

A mother was preparing pancakes for her sons, Kevin and Ryan, ages five and three. The boys began to argue over who would get the first pancake. Their mother saw the opportunity for a moral lesson. "If Jesus were sitting here, He would say, 'Let my brother have the first pancake. I can wait.' "

Kevin turned to his younger brother and said, "Ryan, you be Jesus!"

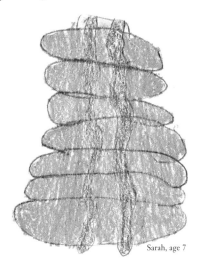

Sarah, age 7

A three-year-old girl walked out of her teenage brother's room laughing. "What's so funny?" her mother asked.

"My name is Carolyn, and Billy doesn't even know it," the child said, giggling. "He said, 'Get out of here, idiot!'"

Ariel, age 9

Seven-year-old Zachary was having dinner with his parents, and as usual they asked him about his day in school. "We had a guy come in and talk to us about sex," Zachary told them proudly.

His parents barely managed to swallow their food without choking. "Well," said his father, "what did he tell you?"

Zachary answered with confidence: "People have to be careful with intersection, and they should always buy condominiums."

Five-year-old Andy overheard his mother talking about changing baby-sitters. "Mommy, are you going to fire Evelyn?" he asked.

"Andy, do you know what 'firing' is?"

"Yes," the child answered. "It's when you don't have a job anymore."

"That's right," replied his mother, surprised.

But the knowledge didn't stop Andy from asking the following question: "Well, are you going to fire her out of a cannon?"

Liviya, age 8

Janey, a four-year-old from Miami, heard from her mother that they were going on a trip to Orlando. "Is that Spanish for Disney World?" she wanted to know.

Three-year-old Pedro, at the beach with his family, was disappointed because there were so few *shells to collect*. His mother explained that it was high tide, but in a few hours it would be low *tide* and they would see many more shells as the ocean receded. Pedro nodded and went to inform his father. "The tide is high, but they're gonna fix it," he reported.

Anthony, age 7

Three kindergartners were talking about the age of their mothers. "My mommy is thirty-four," Adrianne said.

"My mommy is forty," added Therese. She turned to her friend Jessica. "How old is your mommy?"

"I don't know," Jessica answered. "My mommy is quitting her birthdays."

Three-year-old twins were playing an imaginary game of "shoe store." Julian, who was the customer, refused all the imaginary offerings of his brother, Allan. In *exasperation*, Allan-the-salesman blurted out, "Well, what *do* you want?"

Julian replied, "I want them in black."

The salesman's triumphant reply: "Well, we don't have them in **black**!"

Mayra, age 7

Three-year-old Levi had an argument with his father. In frustration the child turned to his mother and asked, "Why did you have to marry a handsome daddy instead of a nice one?"

Three-year-old John was unhappy with his one-year-old *sister*, Catherine. She kept knocking down his block buildings as fast as he could build them. His mother explained that Catherine thought she was playing with her brother, but John had a better *explanation*. "Mommy," he cried, "she just doesn't know the rules!"

Time passed and the children grew. Now three years old, Catherine could participate in many of John's activities. One day as the *children* were playing Candyland, John remarked, "Mom! This is the Catherine I've been waiting for!"

Jarmell, age 7

A mother and her three-year-old son, Timothy, were playing noisily in their front yard.

The father came to the door and asked them to play a bit more quietly so he could get his work done.

"Daddy," replied Timothy indignantly, "I don't _do_ quiet!"

Six-year-old Diana was angry with her family. She packed a few things in her school knapsack and went to the front door. "I am no longer Diana Gold," she announced. "I am Diana White, and I am leaving to find a family that loves me."

Her parents decided to let Diana go. They were on a small island where they knew everyone. Five minutes later, Diana was back.

"Why did you come home?" her sister asked.

Diana shrugged. "I didn't think I could find a family who loves me more than you do."

Three-year-old Will wanted to go to the Bronx Zoo. He *asked* often, but it was a long trip and his parents just didn't have the time to take him there. Will's mother asked the baby-sitter to take him to the Central Park *Zoo* instead. It was considerably smaller but much closer. The baby-sitter agreed and set off with Will on a fine day. When the *mother* returned from work that evening, she asked her son, "Did you do anything special today?"

Will looked at her evenly. "I didn't go to the Bronx Zoo."

Vadim, age 7

Four-year-old Gregory was getting out of the car to go to school.

He turned to give his mother an especially big hug and kiss good-bye.

"There!" he said proudly. "Now you can hold that in your brain all day!"

Albina, age 7

30

Three-year-olds Henry and Tracy shared bathroom time together, as is common in nursery school. Tracy watched with interest as Henry pulled down his pants and urinated. When she went home that day, she told her mother, "Henry has no private parts."

Two five-year-old girls were playing in the schoolyard. Another child ran up to them shouting, "Samantha, Samantha! Ivan is calling you."

Diana, age 8

Obviously unhappy to be disturbed, Samantha glanced up at the messenger. "Just tell him I'm not home," she replied.

Four-year-old Matthew painted a lovely picture at the easel in nursery school one morning, and the teacher hung it on a clothesline to dry. Matthew immediately made a sign for it that read WET PAINT. After about twenty minutes, however, he replaced the sign with another that read DRY PAINT. When his teacher asked him why, he replied, "By the time my mommy gets here, the paint is going to be dry."

Three-year-old Sally's mother had been sick for six months with a terrible case of Lyme disease.

One day Sally became **angry** at a classmate and called him the worst name she could think of:

"You . . . you . . . you *tick*!"

Danielle, age 8

In school one day, four-year-old Davy was bothering Tammy. She decided to tell the teacher. "Davy keeps following me around saying 'A, A, A,' she complained.

"The next time he does, tell him 'B,'" the teacher replied, trying to hide her smile.

Just a minute after the conversation, Davy was back. "A, A, A," he said with a mischievous grin.

"B!" yelled Tammy with the force of a combatant. Surprised, Davy walked away. Tammy looked up at her teacher admiringly. "You know everything," she said with a sigh.

Three-year-old Carrie told her mother, "We went swimming in the little pools at school today."

"You did?" asked her surprised mother. "Did the boys and girls swim together?"

"I don't know," replied Carrie. "We didn't have any bathing suits on."

In a fit of anger, five-year-old Ned threw a chair at a classmate.

When the teacher dashed over to put him in time-out, Ned looked at her incredulously. "But it didn't hit anybody!"

Five-year-old Mark was watching a television show that was almost over. He turned to his mother and asked, "Mommy, if the world ended, would they roll the credits of everybody who ever lived?"

David, age 8

THE SIMSONS

As three-year-old Brian was eating Jell-O, he turned to his mother and asked, "Mommy, do all things start out as Jell-O?"

Tipu, age 7

Five-year-old Albert couldn't get to sleep. He told his father that he was afraid the **monsters** outside would come in and "get" him. "There are no monsters outside," his father replied gently.

"Yes, I can hear them," insisted Albert.

"Those are just **crickets**," his father told him. "Come to the front door with me, and I'll prove it to you."

After the front door had been opened, Albert and his father stood gazing out into the empty night. "I don't see any monsters," said Albert's father.

"Well, I don't see any crickets," answered Albert.

Recognizing that it was a tie, the son and the father went off to sleep.

In kindergarten, five-year-old Jonathan was complaining about life at home with a three-year-old brother. His teacher took him over to a feelings chart that had angry, happy, sleepy, scared, sick, and silly faces on it. The teacher asked Jonathan to point out the face that best described how he felt about his little brother. Jonathan pointed to the circle with the yawning face. "Sleepy, 'cause I'm tired of him."

Harry, age 8

Four-year-old Jose,
on the relatively sad
ending of Disney's
"Pocahontas," when
John Smith returns
to England:

"Well, he can always
visit."

Four-year-old Marianna, whose mother was talking to the teacher, overheard the phrase "children under six." "I'm not under six," Marianna declared, "I'm under five. Next week is my fifth birthday, and then I'll be under six."

Six-year-old Karen asked her mother, "How do you buy a car?"

The mother began to explain about going to a showroom and selecting a model, but the child interrupted. "No, Mommy. I mean, how do you get it on the counter?"

Melanie, age 9

Philip, age three, liked the movie *Pinocchio* so much that he asked his mother to take him again the following day. When his mother asked him how he liked the movie the second time, he replied, "The whale in the first one was better."

Vadim, age 7

Four-year-old Lauren had both an uncle and a classmate named Gerald. Perplexed, she went up to her friend and told him, "You and my uncle are exactly the same except you have a different face."

A teacher was going over the names of animals and their babies with her class of four-year-olds. They went through cow and calf, lion and cub, cat and kitten, and dog and puppy. The teacher decided to ask a hard one. "Who knows what a kid is the baby of?" she inquired.

Susie piped up: "I know! It's a baby grown-up!"

One Christmas morning
three-year-old Wendy looked
under the tree and exclaimed,
"Mommy, look! Santa
Claus has the same
wrapping paper
we have!"

Two-and-a-half-year-old Abby went into a bathroom where there was a bidet. She ran out to her parents and exclaimed, "Wow! A sink for children!"

SANTA HAS THE SAME PAPER

Liviya, age 8

Three-year-old Ari was playing with his grandfather when he suddenly noticed the older man's bald spot. "Grandpa," Ari told him, "you have open hair."

Jacob, age 9

Five-year-old Todd was talking to his mother after he had returned from Sunday school:

"You know those two guys who started the world?"

"Who?" asked his mother.

"You know, Adam and Steve . . ."

Four-year-old Bradley left the classroom for a drink at the water fountain. A minute later a teacher brought him back to class, along with a little girl whose face and blouse were drenched. "This child spit all over my poor Amanda," the teacher said sternly.

Bradley turned to his teacher. "I didn't spit!" he protested.

"You didn't?" his teacher asked.

"No," insisted Bradley. "I spit water."

Seven-year-old Max was told by his parents that they were thinking of having another baby. Max became very upset. "If that happens," he told his parents, "there'll be a rusty old car with a dent and a shiny new red car. Everyone will want to play with the shiny red car, and no one will want to play with the rusty old car anymore. And the rusty old car will be me!"

Mario, age 9

One day three-year-old Jamie heard his mother talking about Grandma Frances. "Where is Grandma Frances?" he wanted to know.

"She died when you were a baby, Jamie," his mother replied gently.

"Really?" Jamie asked. "Who shot her?"

A mother and her three-year-old daughter, Megan, were at a library desk checking out books. As the mother shuffled through her wallet looking for her library card, Megan asked, "Are we going to buy them?"

Her mother said no, and handed her card to the librarian.

"Oh," Megan said knowingly. "We're charging them."

Six-year-old Annie, who had been breast-fed by her mother when she was an infant, asked if she could nurse again. Her mother patiently explained, "The only time mommies can breast-feed is when their children are babies. Otherwise there's no milk."

"That's okay," Annie answered. "I'll take water."

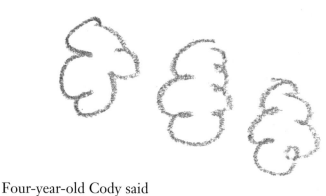

Four-year-old Cody said to his mother, "I can blow bubbles and snap my fingers. I think I'm ready to learn to read."

Jourdan, age 7

Michael, *three years old* **and** *an only child, was about to start his first year of school with his best friend, Arthur. His mother told him that he'd make* **many new friends** *there. He shook his head, saying,* "No more friends, Mommy. There's too much sharing."

Ellie celebrated her fifth birthday at a backyard party with all her friends. It lasted most of the day. Ellie found a quiet moment to go off into a corner and suck her thumb. Ellie's mother, tired from the festivities, saw her daughter and became exasperated. "Ellie, one would think that you could stop sucking your thumb now that you're five!"

"But, Mommy," the child explained, "it's very hard, and I've only been five for one day!"

Liviya, age 8

Seven-year-old Paula and her grandmother were looking through a magazine. "Grandma, I want this bra," said Paula, pointing to an advertisement.

"Well, dear, you have to be a little older and a little more developed," said her grandmother.

Paula protested: "But it says one size fits all!"

Seven-year-old Patricia and five-year-old Peter were talking to their grandparents about a club they had joined that had issued free passes. "It wasn't too much fun," Patricia asserted. "After the first time, I threw my pass away."

Peter piped up, "I would have thrown my pass away, too, but I lost it."

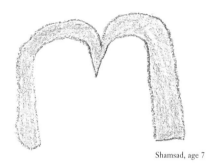

Shamsad, age 7

Three-year-old Chad wanted to tell his grandfather about a conversation he had had with his mother. "Grandpa lives three hundred miles away," explained his mother, "but you can write him a *letter*."

Chad thought carefully for a minute, then made his decision: "I think I'll write him an 'M.'"

Three-year-old Sam told his mother he wanted to be a **doctor** when he grew up. "Really?" said his mom. "What kind of medicine are you going to **practice**?"

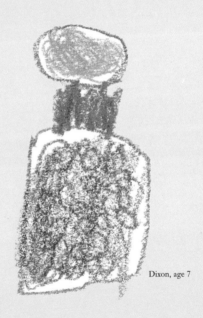

Dixon, age 7

"Sudafed," replied Sam.

Samantha, age 6

Four-year-old Donny, whose mother was pregnant, asked Mary Jane to play **"mommy and daddy"** with him at school. "But I don't know how to play that," said Mary Jane.

"It's easy," Donny told her. "I'll shave and you throw up."

Five-year-old Darren announced to his mother that he was going over to his friend Bobby's house. "Wait a minute. You've never walked there by yourself before. Do you even know where it is?"

"Sure," Darren replied. "It's on a street called Dead End."

"That's not much of a help," his mother told him, trying to hide her smile. "Do you at least know his mother's name?"

Darren thought for a minute. "Same as yours—Mommy."

A mother and grandmother tried to *explain* to four-year-old Taylor that all of the grandmother's brothers were no longer living. They attempted to deliver this information as gently as possible, explaining that the brothers had gone to Heaven to be with God. Taylor asked why.

His grandmother explained that God needed them and that it was their *time* to be with God. Taylor thought about this for a moment, then said, "Oh! You mean they're dead!"

Jacob, age 9

Four-year-old Joseph was making a marble cake with his grandmother. They had put in the eggs, sugar, and flour when Joseph asked, "When do we put in the marbles?"

Jourdan, age 7

At church one Sunday the pastor asked, "How many of you can remember your last home-cooked meal?"

Seven-year-old Barry knew he had the right answer. He looked up at his mother excitedly and said, "At breakfast we had Pop-Tarts!"

A teacher was using pipe cleaners to explain different shapes to her group of four-year-olds.

She showed them that if you stretch a pipe cleaner circle, it will turn into an oval.

"So," one child observed, "an oval is a circle with a stomachache."

Danielle, age 8

On his sixth birthday, Andre was taken to a beautiful lake for a fishing trip. The hike to get there, however, was long and tiring. About halfway into the trip, he declared, "Boy, it's a good thing I'm already six, because if I was still five, I'd be hating this!"

Three-year-old Benjy sat in a New York City taxi with his mother. He pointed to a nearby building. "Our apartment building is *taller* than that," he asserted.

"No, dear, *that* building is taller," said his mother.

"Well, ours has more apartments," he insisted.

"No, I don't really think so," she answered, trying not to dampen his spirit.

Benjy straightened up and made his final and correct **comparison**: "Well," he declared with a wave of his hand, "ours is closer to Jersey."

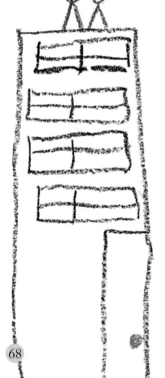

Ashley, age 6

A grandmother was trying to convince her three-year-old granddaughter, Rachel, to come for a visit without her twin brother, Brad. "We can have lots of fun, and you can come over all by yourself," her grandmother told her.

Rachel replied solemnly, "But, Grandma, I don't drive . . ."

Three-year-old Nora went on her first **roller coaster** ride. Afterward, her father asked how she felt. The girl replied, "My stomach feels confused."

Ariel, age 9

Four-year-old Melody, struggling with an **intricate** explanation of menstruation, asked her mother, "Have you gotten your dot yet?"

Two-year-old Sarah leaned over and bit Tommy, her four-year-old brother. He turned to her quite seriously and said, "Sarah, I'm not food."

Roseanna, age 7

A three-year-old city kid went with her parents to the country for the first time. "Look, Gina," her mother said, pointing out the window. "There's a horse!"

The child looked at the animal in wonder and asked, "Where do you put the quarter?"

A family invited an older man to dinner, and, surprisingly, he arrived without his upper *teeth*! After he had eaten and departed, the family discussed the situation.

"Well," suggested seven-year-old Teddy, "maybe he thought it was *informal*."

Ashley, age 6

Five-year-old Kelsey was hungry, and she told her parents in an unusual fashion: "Mommy! The doorbell to my tummy just went off!"

In kindergarten, one little boy had his sixth birthday. The children were discussing how to make "six" using their fingers. Carla said, "I know how!" She held up all the fingers on one hand and the forefinger of the other.

Johnny said, "No. That's not how you make six. This is!" He held up all his fingers on one hand and the other thumb.

The teacher told them that they could use any fingers they wanted to make six.

"No," Johnny told her, holding up his middle finger. "You can't use this one."

On Christmas morning, two-and-a-half-year-old Jeremy unwrapped his first present. It was a musical toy that could be strummed like a guitar, blown like a whistle, and shaken like a tambourine.

As he removed it from the wrapping, he said politely, "Um, just what I always wanted! A thing!"

Four-year-old Andrew had just begun to read. He was riding in the car with his mother one day when he noticed a sign.

"Mom!" he hollered. "That sign said 'do not pass,' and you passed it!"

D.J., almost four, was home when the pastor of his church came to talk to his parents. He listened quietly as they chatted. After the pastor had gone, he asked his mother softly, "Mommy, was that God?"

Eight-year-old Kelly and her seven-year-old brother, Bryce, were taking a car trip with their parents. Kelly said wistfully, "I would love a little brother."

Bryce piped up, "You used to have one, but he's all grown up now."

A nursery school class was talking about balloons. Three-year-old Marissa told her classmates: "Balloons can't talk because they have no face stuff." Everyone agreed.

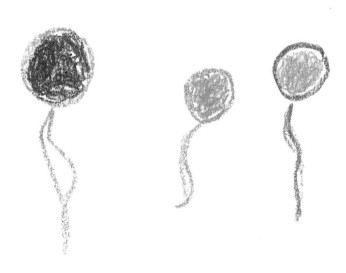

Mario, age 9

Max, age 9

A woman and her three-year-old son were in a doctor's waiting room. An elderly woman in a blue fur *hat* sat next to them. The boy looked at the hat and said, "Lady, you have wonderful *hair*."

She replied, "Why, thank you, dear."

Four-year-old Scott went on a trip with his family. They stayed at a hotel with a view of the ocean and the pool. One night, as Scott was looking out the window, he saw that the ocean was dark but the pool had been lit up for night swimming. Scott observed: "The pool is open but the ocean is closed."

The mother of a four-year-old had this exchange with her son:

"Tad, we are **going** to renovate our kitchen next week. What would you like to have in it?"

"Doughnuts."

Joelissa, age 8

Six-year-old Freddy,
sitting in church
with his grandmoth-
er, turned to her and
announced, "When I
die, I'm not going to
be buried."

"Oh?" asked his
grandmother.

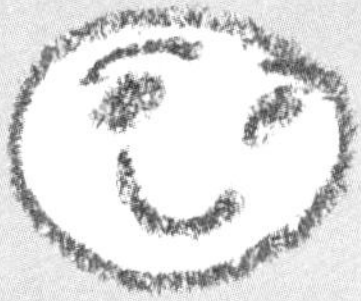

"No," Freddy
replied. "I'm going to
be marinated."

Diana, age 8

Danielle, age 8

Four-year-old Rupert was learning new words daily. As he and his family drove by a park, he pointed to the local swimming pool. "Look, Daddy, there's the swimming pool in the distance!"

His parents hadn't heard him say "distance" before and were very proud. Rupert's father pointed to the other side of the road and asked, "Are those swans in the distance?"

"No," Rupert replied seriously. "They're in the water."

Three-year-old Frankie was on a bus with his mother. "What a cute little girl you are!" said an old woman near him, making a mistake because of Frankie's long hair. Frankie stood up and began to unbutton his pants. "No, I'm a boy. Want to see?"

The mother of four-year-old Adam was having a large dinner party when suddenly her son burst into the dining room in bare feet. "Ow, ow!" he yelled at the top of his lungs. "Mom, I stepped on an old piece of food—again!"

Mirza, age 8

Three-year-old Shelby and five-year-old Eric were having a discussion in the backseat of a car as their family traveled through farm country. "If you put ice and snow on a brown cow's head, you would get chocolate ice cream," said Shelby.

"No, no, silly," corrected her older brother. "You would get chocolate milk."

Three-year-old Katie gave her grandmother a birthday card on which she had **scribbled** a design. Trying to be polite, the grandmother said, "Katie, this is very nice. What does it **say**?"

The child replied with dignity, "Grandma, I can write but I can't read."

A three-year-old boy was learning about **opposites**. He was sitting in church with his mother one day when he began to talk loudly to her. "Ben," she said to him, "in church we whisper."

"AND YELL!" he excitedly replied.

Three-year-old Trisha liked to feed her aunt's goldfish. One day they found the goldfish floating upside down in the tank, lifeless. Before her aunt could explain what had happened, Trisha asked, "Aunt Carol, did the goldfish drown?"

Yarisa, age 7

Leah, age 8

Three-year-old Talia was at the circus with her **father**. She looked around the festively decorated tent and said, "Daddy, I *love* you all the way up to the balloons!"

*E*ach morning as a woman was watering her lawn, her three-year-old neighbor, Brandon, would poke his head through their mutual fence and say hello. One day she saw the little boy at the supermarket shopping with his mother. Brandon pointed to the woman and said, "Hey! How did you get out?"

Shamsad, age 7

Four-year-old Renata and her teacher were walking up the stairs, holding hands. The teacher remarked that walking up stairs is very good for the heart. "The heart is a muscle," she told Renata. "The more you exercise it, the stronger it gets." Renata was silent a moment, then said, "You know, Mrs. Smith, the heart is also for something else."

"What's that?" the teacher asked.

"It's for loving," said the child.

About the Authors

Patti Greenberg Wollman has been an Early Childhood educator for twenty years and is the author of *Behind the Playdough Curtain: A Year in My Life as a Preschool Teacher*. She is the director of the Nursery School at Habonim. Merril Feinstein-Feit is an Early Childhood teacher at a private school in Manhattan. She also conducts teacher training workshops. The authors live in New York City with their husbands and children.

The authors would love to see your favorite kid-related anecdotes for possible use in future books. You can write to the authors at:

DaMama1@aol.com
or
merril@heschel.org

or in care of:
Golden Books
888 Seventh Avenue
New York, NY 10106